A Big Day in Nicodemus

by Gloria Gorman
illustrated by L. Epstein

Harcourt

Orlando   Boston   Dallas   Chicago   San Diego

Visit *The Learning Site!*

www.harcourtschool.com

"Justus! Hurry up!" called Ruby. "The game starts in an hour. Don't you want to get a good seat? I had to pay for these tickets in installments! And I've never paid for anything in installments before! I don't want to miss any part of this game!"

"I'm trying to hurry up," Justus called back. "But Earl is hiding under the porch, and I can't get him out. That dog seems to think he's a rabbit! Why else do you think he burrowed himself into that hole he dug?"

"Oh, Justus, don't be silly. I doubt if he's burrowed into a hole under there. Maybe he's burying something or digging something up. In any case, let's get going. It'll be very crowded today, and I want to get a good seat. If we just leave, maybe Earl will follow us. You know how he enjoys these baseball games."

"Ok, Ruby. Maybe you're right. But I wish I had found my baseball glove. You never know when you might have a chance to catch a ball that's hit all the way to the bleachers. I just can't imagine where that glove could be. I was just using it last week at the neighborhood baseball game," Justus said.

Justus and Ruby headed out to the baseball field. As soon as Earl noticed they were leaving, he came out from under the porch and followed them. Between his teeth, he held Justus's baseball glove.

"Hey, Earl," said Justus when he saw the glove. "Where did you get that? I've been looking all over for it."

Earl just barked as if he had played the best joke of his life.

By the time Justus, Ruby, and Earl got to the baseball field, a big crowd had already gathered. There seemed to have been an exodus of all the people of Nicodemus from the town to the ball field. In fact, there must have been an exodus from several neighboring towns as well. The stands on both sides were full.

A large group stood at one end of the field. Even though there wasn't enough space in the stands, it was clear that nobody wanted to miss the game.

Earl found a few dog buddies and went off to play dog games. Whenever there was a baseball game in Nicodemus, the dogs enjoyed it just as much as the people did. There was a party feeling in the air, and the dogs seemed to sense it. Baseball day could just as well have been designated "Dog Fun Day" as far as the dogs were concerned.

Justus and Ruby migrated to the bleachers. It would still be thirty minutes until the first pitch was thrown. The stands had never filled up this early before, but there was a good reason for all this interest in the game.

Today was the day the great Satchel Paige was coming to play baseball in Nicodemus. The home-town team, the Nicodemus Blues, would get a chance to bat against the greatest pitcher the world had ever seen. Even if Satchel hadn't been officially designated that, everyone knew it was true.

At last, the players started drifting out onto the field. When Satchel himself showed up, he walked slowly, as usual. He had once said that to keep himself young, he would "keep the juices flowing by jangling around gently" as he moved—and Satchel certainly never seemed to be in a hurry.

Satchel's team, the Kansas City Monarchs, was up first. In a way, everyone wanted it to be the other way around. They wanted to see Satchel pitch! That was the main reason they had come.

The top half of the first inning seemed to take
forever. The fans were getting restless. Finally,
the visiting team got their third out, and the
Nicodemus Blues were up at bat. Satchel Paige
walked slowly to his place on the pitcher's mound.
He seemed to be following his own advice to
"avoid running at all times."

He prepared for his first pitch. A hush fell over the crowd as he began his famous windup. It was hard to see anything but his legs and arms. He spun his arm forward and backward half a dozen times. Then he leaned way back and stuck his size-fourteen foot in the air. At last his arm came forward. The rest of him followed, and the ball flew by the batter. "Strike one!" yelled the umpire.

"Next one will be my 'bee ball,'" shouted Satchel. It wasn't unusual for Satchel to tell the batter exactly what was coming. Most batters couldn't hit what he threw anyway.

Justus leaned over to Ruby. "That's the ball that will always be where he wants it to be," he said.

"I know what it is, Justus. I know more about Satchel Paige than you do! It's also called a 'bee ball' because it seems to hum as it travels."

They both watched as the second pitch shot over
the plate. "Strike two!" yelled the umpire.

Satchel wound up for pitch number three and
threw a curve ball. "Strike three!" yelled the umpire.

During the bottom of the second inning, Satchel
Paige threw three of his most well-known pitches.

He threw the first batter a "jump ball," which
seemed to hop around a bit in the air as it
approached the plate.

He threw what he called a "bat dodger" to the second batter, and then he threw what the batters called a "pea ball." The pea ball got its name because the ball seemed to get smaller as it neared the plate, since it was moving so fast. Satchel had thrown six strikes in a row. Two batters were out, and neither had even come close to hitting the ball.

As the third batter came up to the plate, Satchel gestured to everyone on his team to sit down on the field. The outfielders sat down on the grass. The infielders sat down on the dirt. The only player on his feet was Satchel Paige. He was so sure that he'd strike out the next batter that he thought he'd give his teammates a chance to relax.

He wasn't wrong. Three pitches later, the umpire yelled, "Strike three!"

"At this rate, this will be a fast game," said Ruby.

"You're right about that," said Justus. "I guess I won't be catching a foul ball today. Nobody's going to hit one! Still, I'm really glad we came. This is the most exciting day of my life!"

"Mine, too!" said Ruby. "So far, anyway!"